Blood Behind the Mask

Alisa McMillan

ISBN: 978-1-969880-09-4

Dedication

I dedicate this book to my Husband Traig McMillan, and my Children Alisa McMillan, Dashawn McMillan, Nayquan West, Jasmine Simpson, Keith West jr, Traig McMillan, Traig McMillan Jr., Janice Martin, Rashead Washington and my dad, Gregory Searls and my grandchildren. I love you all.

Acknowledgment

I would like to acknowledge my Dad Gregory Don Searls for inspiration after my mother's passing and some loss of vision to keep pushing.

Contents

About the Author

Alisa is a mother of 9 children and partially blind. She loves to write and enjoy horror movies, and this inspired her to write one on her own. She is also spiritual and believes in a higher power. She wants everyone to enjoy her work.

Character Description

GREGORY	White male, age seventeen Serious attitude. Brenda's boyfriend.
MAX	White male, age eighteen. Playful person. Amy's boyfriend.
BOB	Black male, age eighteen. Comedian. Brenda's boyfriend.
LORRAINE	Black female, age nineteen. Conceited.
CRYSTAL	White female, age seventeen. Funny disposition. Steve's girlfriend.
STEVE	White male, twenty years old. Serious attitude. Crystal's boyfriend.
ALICE	White female, age nineteen. Death Jones's niece. Curious and concerned. Dave's girlfriend.
DAVE	White male, age nineteen. Scary personality. Concerned individual. Alice's boyfriend.
LAURY	White female, age fifty-three. Experienced. Tommy's mother and Alice's grandma. Person to play her hopefully Jamie Lee Curtis. (Not too many parts for her.)
TOMMY	White male, age thirty-five. Concerned individual, Alice's father,

POLICE OPERATOR   Laury's son. Business man for
                                         computers.

POLICE OPERATOR   Black female, age thirty.
                                         experienced.

SHERRIFF   White male, age forty-five. On his
                                         job and well experienced.

DEPUTY   White male, age thirty-five. Goofy
                                         type of person.

POLICE OFFICER #1   White male, thirty-one years old.
                                         Serious about his job.

POLICE OFFICER #2   White male, thirty-three years old.
                                         Serious disposition.

MR. ROBINSON   White male, thirty-four years old.
                                         Teacher at Haddonfield Hight School.
                                         Well dressed.

BRENDA   White female, age seventeen.
                                         Gregory's girlfriend.

FATAL FOE

DEATH JONES

GREGORY   White male, age eighteen. Brenda's
                                         boyfriend.

AMY   White female, age eighteen. Max's
                                         girlfriend.

Scene 1

Alice is sitting in class. The teacher, Mr. Robinson, reminds the class to have their projects done by next week.

(Raising her hand) Alice: Mr. Robinson

Mr. Robinson: Yes, Alice. What is it?

Alice: Can I do my project on horror?

Mr. Robinson: Yes, Alice, but please make it interesting.

The class is laughing. As they laugh, the bell rings to end the day.

Alice grabs her books and walks down the hall. Alice bumps into Dave, dropping her books. Dave leans down, picking up Alice's books. Dave gives Alice her books.

Dave: Hey, baby! How was class?

Alice: All right, I guess.

Dave: Are you still going on the trip next week?

Alice: I'm sure I will be there.

Dave: I sure hope so.

Alice: Nothing is stopping me from going to Camp Crystal Lake. I've been dying to get there.

Dave: Well, if all is good, your dream will be fulfilled.

Alice (in a hurry): Well, let me go home. My father will be worried if I don't hurry.

Dave kisses Alice on her cheek.

Dave (waving): See you later, Alice.

Alice walks up the hallway. Almost at the front of the door, she bumps into Amy.

Amy (stopping Alice): Alice, you're in such a rush.

Alice (stops to talk to Amy): Yes, Amy, Dave and I were chatting. Now I really have to go home.

Amy: Are you still going to Camp Crystal Lake next week?

Alice (smiling): Yes we are. Are you going?

Amy (looking sad): No, my parents won't allow me to go. They're spooked out on that Fatal crap.

Alice (looking concerned): Fatal has been dead for almost a decade. I'm not worried about him. It's the people alive you have to worry about.

Amy (turning her back and waving): Well, I'll talk to you later.

Alice: Okay, good-bye.

Alice proceeds out of the school and walks down the steps of the school. She notices a car; it's her friends Max, Brenda, and Gregory.

Scene 2

Gregory (looking happy): Hey, Alice. Alice: What is it?

Gregory: Do you want a ride?

Alice: Sure, as long as you haven't been drinking.

Gregory: Alice, you're crazy!

Alice opens the car door and gets in. Gregory pulls off. driving Alice to her house.

Alice: Hey, where were you guys headed?

Brenda: Girl, we were just riding around thinking about what we're going to do tonight.

Max: Alice, I thought you graduated out of Haddonfield High School.

Alice: I'm a senior, I'll graduate this year.

Scene 3

The car pulls up to Alice's house. Alice gets out of the car. Alice leans her head in the car and gives Brenda a piece of paper.

Brenda (giving a questioning look): What is this? Alice: My new phone number. Call me tonight. Brenda: Okay. I sure will.

Alice walks up to her front door of her home. Dropping her books on the couch, she proceeds to the kitchen. Her father Tommy is in the kitchen.

Scene 4

Tommy (looking surprised): Hi, Honey.

Alice: Hi, Dad.

Tommy is sitting at the table drinking coffee. As Alice prepares a sandwich and cup of milk, she sits at the table and takes a bite of her sandwich. Tommy takes another sip of his hot coffee.

Tommy: Alice, baby, how was school today?

Alice: A drag as usual.

Tommy (looking concerned): Alice, education is the best thing for you. You need to stop hanging around that crazy guy Dave.

Alice: Dad I love Dave. Dave hasn't smoked pot in months.

Tommy (aggravated): Once a pothead, always a pothead.

Alice: Dad, that just isn't true. Everyone needs change and can change.

Tommy: Well, your grandmother and I feel you need to hang with a better crowd.

Alice (looking upset): Grandma is never pleased with anything I do.

Tommy: Alice, please don't get upset. We love you. We're just concerned about your future.

Alice (yelling): I'm a big girl now, Dad. Please let me live my life.

Tommy (yelling back): Baby...

Alice storms out of the kitchen and runs upstairs to her room.

She's lying on her bed, and the phone rings.

Scene 5

Tommy (yelling): I got it, Alice.

Tommy picks up the phone. Tommy: Hello?

Laury (Tommy's mom): Hello, son, how are you feeling today?

Tommy: Not so good. Your granddaughter is out of control.

Laury: Well, our family has been like that for centuries. Just take a look at how Death Jones was. You couldn't find a crazier guy.

Tommy (looking upset): Mom, please! Stop mentioning his name. I hate the sound of it.

Laury: Well, son, he's gone for good, so you're right. Our lives must go on. By the way, where is Alice?

Tommy: She's upstairs; she's upset with me.

Laury: Why?

Tommy: I just advised her to find a new crowd to be around. She will not accept that.

Laury: Well, you were the same way when you were younger. She'll grow out of it.

Tommy: Well, I hope so.

Laury: Don't worry, son; she will.

Tommy: Okay, Mom; I'll talk to you later Laury: All right, I love you.

Tommy and Laury hang up the phones. Tommy walks out of the kitchen and picks his jacket up off the couch.

Scene 6

Tommy (yelling): Alice, I'll see you later. I have a meeting to go to.

Alice walks to the head of the steps and looks down at her father.

Alice (smiling): Okay, Dad, I'll see you later. Tommy: Remember, don't let anyone into my home.

Alice: Come on, Dad.

Tommy: Let me go, honey, I'm running late.

Scene 7

Tommy walks out the door and locks it. Alice runs downstairs to the kitchen and picks up the phone. She dials out on the phone.

Dave: Hello?

Alice (looking happy): Hi, baby! What are you doing?

Dave: I'm just finishing up some homework.

Alice: Well, when you finish your homework, please come over to my house.

Dave (smiling): Are you kidding? Where's your old man?

Alice: He's gone. He won't be back until midnight. Dave (excited): Jesus! That's great.

Alice: So I'll see you tonight.

Dave: You sure will.

Alice: Okay, let me take a shower and freshen up.

Dave: All right, see you later.

Alice: Okay, good-bye.

Alice hangs up the phone. She opens her closet in the living room and picks out a pair of shoes. She heads upstairs to her room and opens the closet to her room. As she rests her shoes o the floor, she picks out a housecoat and a towel. Alice lets down her hair and proceeds to the shower.

Scene 8

In The Town Of Haddonfield.

In Haddonfield cemetery lays the body of Death Jones. It lies headless and lonely. The graveyard is still and quiet, all except for the groundskeeper. He's drinking whiskey, talking to himself, and is very intoxicated. The groundskeeper is walking to Death Jones's gravesite and looking at the stone that reads: Death Jones. The groundskeeper digs up the gravesite until he sees a wooden coffin. He wipes the sweat off the side of his face and jumps down, opening up the coffin. Maggots are crawling over Death Jones's body. Tossing the body over his shoulders, he proceeds to walk to the mausoleum. There he places Death Jones's body and head on the table. The groundskeeper takes a sip of whiskey, looking down at Death Jones. Groundskeeper (intoxicated): Damn! You're one ugly motherfucker.

The groundskeeper takes another sip of his whiskey. The groundskeeper puts his bottle down and pulls out a package. He opens the package and pulls out its contents, which include a needle and thread with some peroxide solution. He pours the solution on the ripped neck of Death Jones. The groundskeeper is sewing his head onto his body. Death Jones's head is completely back on his body. As the groundskeeper puts up the utensils used on Death Jones, a bolt of lightning strikes Death Jones in the chest.

The groundskeeper is unaware of this. Death Jones's eyes open. The groundskeeper has his back turned, cleaning the utensils and his hands. Death Jones is behind the groundskeeper standing still. The groundskeeper turns around and looks scared but surprised. Death Jones takes both hands and grabs the groundskeeper's neck, choking him to death. Death Jones then picks up a scalpel that lies nearby. Death Jones stabs the groundskeeper in the eye with the scalpel.

Scene 9

In the town of Williamsburg

Back into town... Alice's doorbell rings. Alice runs downstairs to answer the door.

Alice: Who is it?

Dave stands outside the door with some flowers behind his back.

Alice opens the door and sees Dave.

Alice (looking happy): Come in, Dave.

Dave (showing the flowers): Here, these are for you.

Alice (looking surprised): Oh Dave, you didn't have to buy me flowers.

Dave: Yes I did! You're my love.

Dave and Alice are sitting on the couch. Dave puts the television on.

Dave (looking concerned)

Alice: Every year just before Halloween, I get nervous.

Dave (wondering): Why?

Alice: I'm not sure it'll be a good idea to tell you. I don't want to run you away.

Dave: Alice, nothing or no one can take my heart from you.

Alice (looking into Dave's eyes): Are you sure? Dave holds Alice's chin.

Dave (looking sincere): I'm sure.

Alice: Well, all right, have you heard about the psycho killer Death Jones?

Dave (looking surprised): You mean that masked guy that was trying to kill his entire family?

Alice: Yes!

Dave (with a questioning look): What does that have to do with you?

Alice: Well, that's just it. He's my uncle.

Dave's mouth is wide open, as he looks surprised.

Alice (looks concerned): Dave, are you all right?

Dave (still in shock): Yes, that's quite surprising,

Alice (looking afraid): Please don't tell anyone.

Dave: Don't worry, that will be our secret-and besides, he's dead anyway. He can't harm you or your family anymore.

Alice: Baby, I love you, and you're absolutely right. He can't harm me.

Dave holds Alice in his arms.

Dave: Why didn't you tell me before?

Alice: Would it have made a difference?

Dave: Yes, I could have given you some comfort about the situation. I didn't want you to feel bad. That makes me feel bad.

Alice: Well, it's great to have someone by my side. I get tired of my father always questioning me.

Dave: About what?

Alice: My daily activities

Dave: I know it's just hard to accept.

Scene 10

Dave hugs Alice, and they began kissing. Back in town Max, Brenda, and Gregory are riding in the car. Gregory drops Brenda off at her house.

Gregory: Brenda, please be ready at 8:00 tonight. I'll pick you up.

Brenda: Gregory, you just be there.

Gregory: I'll be there at 8:00 tonight

Brenda: Okay, you guys. See you tonight Gregory pulls off in the car.

Max: Man that's a beautiful woman you have.

Gregory: How beautiful?

Max: So beautiful I want to fuck her.

Gregory hits Max's shoulder. Greg and Max start laughing. Greg pulls up to Maxs house and drops Max off.

Gregory: Max, please be ready at 8:00 tonight. We have to pick up Amy and Brenda.

Max: Okay, I'll see you tonight.

Gregory pulls off in the car and drives home. Gregory gets out of his car and opens his house door. Just as he does, the phone rings.

Gregory runs in to answer the phone.

Gregory: Hello, who is this?

Dave: Me, man, it's Dave.

Gregory: What's up, Dave? What are you doing?

Dave: Well, I called to see what you and Max had planned for tonight. Alice and me are at her place. Her father won't be home until midnight.

Gregory: Well, we're going camping with the girls tonight in the woods. We'll have a little booze and food. We're looking to have lots of fun.

Dave: Well, I wish you guys the best of luck. I will stay in the house with Alice.

Gregory: Okay, man, let me take my shower and get ready, I have to pick everyone up.

Dave and Gregory hang up the phones. Dave embraces Alice.

Dave: Well, it looks like we have the night to ourselves.

Alice: Where are those guys going?

Dave: Camping

Alice: I hope that's a good idea.

Scene 11

Amy gets out the shower and calls Brenda. Amy: Hello, Brenda.

Brenda: Yes, how are you?

Amy: Well, I just got out of the shower. I will be ready in one hour.

Brenda: Well, I'm ready to go. By the way, how much do you like Max?

Amy: I love Max. Brenda, I just haven't told him.

Brenda: Well, you'll have your chance tonight. Amy: I sure will.

Brenda: Okay, Amy, see you later.

Scene 12

Gregory gets out the shower and gets dressed. His phone rings.

Gregory: Hello, who is it?

Max: It's me, Max! Are you ready?

Gregory: Yes, I will be at your house in five minutes.

Max: Okay, see ya then.

Gregory puts on his sneakers and walks out of the house. He jumps into his car and drives off. He drives up to Max's house and blows the horn. Max peeps out the door.

Gregory: Come on, man, jump in. Let's get the booze and the girls.

Max: Let's go

Max jumps in the vehicle and they drive off. Gregory turns up the music, and they're rocking back and forth singing hard rock tunes.

Max (pointing his finger): Greg, stop at this store, and let me get some beers.

Max goes into the store and purchases two cases of Coors beer and walks back to the car, and then Max gets in the car.

Gregory: You straight?

Max: Yes, I have the beers. Now let's get the girls.

Gregory pulls up to Brenda's house, blowing his horn. Brenda comes down her steps with a red silk dress on.

Brenda: It's about time you damn jerks showed up. I was getting tired.

Max: You look it

Brenda (upset): Max, fuck off, you're such an ass some days.

Gregory: You guys knock it off. Let's go get Amy and have a good night tonight.

Brenda sits in the car putting on her cherry lipstick. As Gregory drives up to the side of Amy's house, Gregory blows the horn. Amy runs out of her house.

Max: Hello, baby.

Amy: I thought you guys forgot about me.

Max: How could I? Come on, jump in.

Amy gets in the back seat of the car with Max. Gregory pulls off, headed to the woods.

Gregory (looking through the rearview mirror): Max, won't you stop player hating?

Amy: Don't worry, Max, I have something for you.

The group starts laughing. Gregory pulls up to the sign that says Haddonfield Forest.

Scene 13

Int... HADDONFIELD FOREST.

The group gets out of the car. Max grabs the cases of beer, holding Amy with his other arm. Gregory stops walking and goes back to the car to get his flashlight.

Brenda (impatient): Gregory, would you come on?

Gregory: Yes, honey, I'm on my way.

Gregory closes the car door and walks toward Brenda, hugging her as they walk through the woods. The group is now in the middle of the woods, where they start a fire and sit down in a circle. Each person takes a can of beer and toasts to an evening together.

Amy: Max, may I ask you a question?

Max: Yes, Amy, what is it?

Amy (looking curious): Why do you spend most of your time with your friends and not me?

Max: Aren't I with you now?

Amy: Yes, but that's not what I mean.

Max (very upset): Well, what the hell is it?

Amy (looking convinced): You see! You get so upset, and all I ever wanted was to be alone with you.

Max (getting up from sitting): Look, Amy, I'm tired of your little attitude. It's time you grow up.

Amy (very upset): Well, if that's how you feel, then forget you.

Max (yelling): Fine!

Gregory (yelling): Will you guys cut it out!

Amy: No! He's right, it's off!

Scene 14

Amy gets up and walks deep into the woods by herself. Death Jones is close by, watching Amy. Amy rests on a nearby tree. Death Jones pulls out his machete and slices Amy's throat. Blood is squirting everywhere as Amy's eyes close. Amy is now dead, standing slumped on the tree.

INT...At the camping site

Scene 15

Back at the camping site, the group is wondering where Amy is and why hasn't she come back.

Gregory (yelling): Max! You know how Amy is. Why did you have to piss her off?

Max (looking with sympathy): I'm sorry. I'm just not used to girls with so many questions.

Brenda: Well, I'm going to find my friend. Fuck you, Max.

Scene 16

Brenda gets up, walking through the woods and looking for Amy. Brenda calls out Amy's name repeatedly. Brenda finally sees Amy slumped over on a tree. Death Jones jumps in front of Brenda with a long spear in his hand. Death Jones shoves the spear through Brenda's mouth as she opens it to scream. The spear enters Brenda's mouth and goes through the back of her head. Death Jones then pulls the spear out with half of Brenda's brains on it. Brenda's body droops, and Death Jones picks up her body and walks into the woods with it.

Scene 17

INT... Back at the campfire

Max and Gregory are getting impatient waiting for the girls.

Max (nervous): Damn, I wish I hadn't pissed Amy off. I mean, I could go for a blowjob now.

Gregory: Well, congratulations. You fucked up, Max.

Max (curious): Where the hell are the girls anyway?

Gregory: Yes, it's taking Brenda a little longer than expected.

Max: Well, I'm going to look for both of them. Greg. you stay here in case they come back.

Gregory (looking nervous): Don't disappear on me, Max. There's some weird shit going down. I just can't put my finger on it.

Max (yelling): Will you chill out, Greg! You had a little too much to drink.

Gregory: It's not that, Max. It just seems a little weird, that's all.

Max gets up and takes another swallow of his beer. Max throws the beer can down and walks off into the woods. Max notices Amy laid up on the tree.

Max: There you are, Amy. What's wrong with you? I'm sorry for what I said back at the campfire.

Max walks right up on Amy and sees Amy's throat slashed. Max screams aloud, "Oh my God!" Max starts dashing through the woods, running and running halfway through the woods. Death Jones jumps out of a tree. Now Death Jones is standing in front of Max. Max's eyes are wide open. Max is in shock. Death Jones takes his knife and plunges it into Max's heart. Max's heart comes out of his chest when Death Jones takes his knife out, and it is still beating on the knife. Death Jones takes the knife and waves it very hard, flinging the heart into a nearby bush.

Scene 18

INT... Back at the campfire

Gregory is nervous and feeling empty. Gregory picks up his flashlight and goes into the woods with caution. Gregory gets halfway into with woods and finds Max's body lying there with a hole in his chest. Gregory turns around quickly. Gregory is running to reach his car. Gregory reaches his car and gets in. Gregory starts the car. Crying and in panic, Gregory drives off.

Gregory drives to the sheriff's office. Gregory jumps out and runs to see the sheriff.

Scene 19

Gregory (hysterical): Sir, me and my friends were at Haddonfield Forest and....

Sheriff (holding his hand up): Wait a minute, slow down. What were you saying?

Gregory: My friends are all dead!

Sheriff: What?

Gregory: Yes, we were in the forest, and one by one they went into the woods and never came back out.

Sheriff (with a questioning look): Well, how do you know they're all dead?

Gregory: Because I went to see what happened to Max, and I found him lying there dead.

Sheriff: Oh my God! Well, boy, you just take my deputy and me to this place.

The sheriff gets up from the desk and radios the deputy. The deputy walks into the office.

Sheriff: We have a situation at Haddonfield Forest. Get the squad car and let's get going.

Deputy: Yes sir.

The deputy walks out of the office and starts up the car. The sheriff looks at Gregory and grabs his shoulder, hugging him. As they both walk out of the office, they get into the patrol car. The deputy drives off.

Sheriff: Boy, this better not be a prank. It's kind of late, and you interrupted my coffee.

Gregory: I have better things to do besides making shit up.

Sheriff: Who were all the people with you? And what are their addresses?

Gregory: Well, it was Max from 110 Cedar Lane, Brenda, who was my girlfriend, from 220 Brick Road, and Amy from 111 Cherry Street.

Scene 20

As Gregory tells this to the sheriff, the sheriff is jotting it down on his pad. The deputy pulls up to Haddonfield Park. Everyone gets out of the car. As Gregory leads the way, Gregory shows the sheriff where they were camping,

Sheriff (looking down at the beer cans): Damn, you guys had a lot to drink!

Gregory leads them off into the woods. Max's body still lies there on the ground. The sheriff bends down and looks at Max.

Sheriff: Damn, looks like some maniac is loose around here.

Gregory: I still haven't found the rest of my friends.

Sheriff: Well, let's walk through these woods and see what we find.

Deputy: Sir, you don't think Death Jones is back?

Sheriff (looking amazed): Don't be an asshole, boy! Death Jones is dead and gone.

Gregory: You mean that creep Death Jones?

Deputy: Yes, boy, but the sheriff says he's not alive.

Gregory: Well then, who's doing this shit?

Sheriff: I don't know, but it's my duty to find out.

As the group walks on, they see Amy in the tree. They walk upon her and realize she's dead too.

Gregory (in shock): My God! My God! Amy!

The sheriff radios for the mortuary van. He embraces Gregory, who is now startled. As they walk back through the woods, they notice a leg hanging out of a bush

Gregory: Oh God! It's Brenda!

Sheriff: You stay here, boy. Let me take a look.

The sheriff looks at Brenda and walks back to the deputy and Gregory.

Sheriff: Deputy, please take Mr. Gregory home, and I will wait here for the meat wagon to come. Call these kids' parents and inform them of what happened.

Scene 21

Back into town...

Alice and Dave are in the Dodge van picking up Crystal and Lorraine. They're going on their trip to Camp Crystal Lake. They still have to pick up Steve and Bob.

Dave: I sure wonder how Max and Gregory are doing. They said they were headed to Haddonfield Park to have some fun with the girls.

Alice: Well, we are going to have fun, and our trip will be beautiful.

Dave (looking at Alice): I hope so.

Alice (seeming upset): Will you stop that?

Dave (smiling): I'm just kidding....

Dave blows the horn. Lorraine and Crystal start running out of the house and jump into the jeep.

Crystal: Okay, you guys, where can I put my bags? Dave (pointing to the back): In the back seat.

Crystal: Thanks, by the way. Where are those two knuckleheads?

Alice: Who?

Crystal: Bob and Steve! Who else?

Alice: Well, they're both at Bob's house. That's where we're headed now.

Dave pulls off, driving the jeep.

Scene 22

INT... Back at the sheriff's office

The sheriff walks in and throws his hat down hard on his desk; he looks at the wall in dismay.

Deputy: Sheriff, I phoned all the parents of those kids. The parents are on their way down to Haddonfield Hospital.

Sheriff (with a smirk): Good job. Now, if you don't mind, take this young fellow home.

Deputy: Yes, sir.

Gregory gets up; he still has nothing to say. He walks out and gets into the car as the deputy gets in too. The deputy drives Gregory to his front door.

Deputy: So, Greg, we will hold your car for you until you feel well enough to pick it up. I know you're in shock. Just try to take it easy.

The deputy pulls up to Gregory's house. Gregory is sitting in shock.

Deputy (parting Gregory's leg): Okay, Greg, you're home.

Gregory (snapping out of a trance): Thanks, Sir.

Deputy: No problem. Just get some rest. We'll be contacting you again.

Gregory gets out of the car, slamming the door. He runs up the stairs of his home and opens the front door.

Scene 23

INT... Back into town

Dave pulls up to Steve's house and blows his horn. Bob looks out the door.

Bob (peeking out): We're coming! Dave: I bet you are. You faggots. Bob: Knock it off, Dave.

Bob and Steve run to the jeep and get in. Steve: Hello, everyone. How is everyone? Lorraine: We were fine until you showed up.

The group starts laughing as Dave pulls off, starting the long trip to Camp Crystal Lake.

INT... On the road to Camp Crystal Lake

The group is driving up the road in a 2002 Dodge Ram. Crystal and Bob are partying, drinking, and talking about their famous trip to camp Crystal Lake.

Crystal (excited): You guys sure will love our vacation. After all, it's Halloween, and we're going to have so much fun that we'll wake up the dead, including that creep Fatal Foe.

Bob (looking scared): Please don't say that name. It gives me the chills.

Steve (with pride): Bob, you sure are chicken shit. Hold on to your trousers. We're going to have fun.

Dave (questionable): How much fun do you jerks think we're going to have? Just knowing that Alice is Death Jones' niece is unbearable!

Alice (upset): You listen, you piece of shit! Nobody knows this but us. Not even Death Jones knows he has relatives alive.

Scene 24

The van pulls up to the cabin in Camp Crystal Lake.

Alice: You guys, let's unpack and go for a swim.

The group follows, unpacking their belongings and loading them into the three-room cabin. Dave and Alice enter the room.

Alice: Dave, baby, did you have to tell everyone about my uncle Death Jones?

Dave (caresses Alice): Baby, I love you. I didn't mean any harm. It's Halloween tomorrow, and the thought just gives me the chills.

Alice: Baby, I hope we can enjoy ourselves and leave those old haunted memories behind.

Someone knocks on the door.

Alice (surprised): Who is it?

Lorraine: It's me. Are you guys ready?

Dave: We'll be right back!!

Lorraine and the group head outside toward the water. Everyone except Lorraine gets in the water. Dave: What's up, Lorraine? Are you chicken shit?

Lorraine: No, I'll just wait here for you guys.

As the group swims, the clouds get dark, and a streak of lightning hits the metal part of the boat and hits the ground two feet from Lorraine. Lorraine jumps back as the ground opens up. Underneath, Fatal Foe has received electric volts, which bring him back to life.

Lorraine: Come on, you guys. It's going to be a terrible storm.

The group dashes for their clothing. Everyone is getting dressed as the rain comes down hard. The group starts back to the cabin, except Lorraine.

Dave (with a questioning look): Lorraine, what's wrong?

Lorraine (snapping out of a trance): Nothing, I mean, I'm sure I just felt movement in the ground. Look at this hole. The lighting was really strong.

Bob: You guys are too curious. Come on, you guys. Last one back to the cabin is a dead man.

The group starts jogging back to the cabin. Everyone is sitting in a circle on the floor, drinking beer.

Dave: What are you guys' plans for tomorrow?

Bob: Well, Steve and I thought we'd go fishing to give the girls something to cook for the party.

Dave: What party?

Steve: What do you mean what party? Tomorrow is Halloween, and we're going to have fun.

Steve takes another sip of his beer.

Lorraine: Yes, me and the girls will go into town and pick up beers and groceries.

The phone rings

Bob (yelling): Alice, it's for you

Alice: Who is it?

Bob: It's your father, Tommy.

Alice gets up to answer the phone. Alice picks up the phone

Alice (smiling): Hello, Dad.

Tommy: Hi, sweetheart. It seems like you're having a nice time. Well, I'm sorry to inform you, but Death Jones's body is missing, and we can't find his head either.

Alice (looks worried): What do you mean? And what does that have to do with me?

Tommy (trying to be of comfort): Well, Death Jones thinks I'm dead, and I just want to be sure you're safe. He's not in Haddonfield. I mean, we can't find him anywhere.

Alice (upset): Dad, I really have to go now. This is ridiculous. Please call me the moment you hear something.

Tommy: I will, baby. Just keep safe.

Alice hangs up the phone and enters the living room.

Dave (puzzled): Honey, what was that about?

Alice: They can't find Death Jones' body anywhere, and they believe he's alive.

Bob (excited): That creep was always hard to kill. He just didn't have a good ass kicking yet.

Group: Bob, shut up!

Fatal Foe is outside in the weeds. Lorraine: You guys, did you hear that?

Steve (upset): Jesus shit! Don't tell me you guys are going to be spooked out of your minds.

Lorraine: No. I'm serious, you guys, something strange happened by the water. It was like something was alive under the ground. Now I hear footsteps.

Bob (very upset): Bitch, did you take your medication?

Dave (yelling): Enough, you guys. Let's go to bed. We have a long day tomorrow.

The group heads upstairs to their rooms

INT... Back in Haddonfield...

Two lovers are in a car, kissing. Death Jones pushes his hand through the window and grabs the guy out, ripping his entire head off with a short machete. As the girl screams, Death Jones breaks her neck, squeezing it until her eyeballs fall out. Death Jones pushes her body out of the car. He drives off with the dead couple's vehicle.

INT... Back at Camp Crystal Lake...

Back at the cabin, everyone is sound asleep, waiting for the big holiday that awaits them. Steve and Crystal are awoken by a sudden noise downstairs.

Crystal (sitting up): Steve, honey, did you hear that?

Steve: Yes, I did. It may be someone getting something to eat.

Crystal (unbelieving): No, Steve, everyone had enough to eat. Please check downstairs and see who it may be.

Steve (upset): Damn! Life isn't fair. I went to sleep with a hard on and woke up just before I had a wet dream.

Steve gets out of bed and goes downstairs. As he enters the kitchen, he flicks on the light. He notices large mud prints of someone's foot and an awful odor.

Steve: Damn, what the hell is this?

Fatal Foe is right behind Steve with a metal arrow. Steve turns around. Before he can yell, the arrow is pushed through his chest, and his heart is pulled out of his chest, still beating on the tip of the arrow.

Then Fatal Foe takes his short machete and chops Steve's head in half, leaving one side of it on his neck with his brain pulsing.

Crystal (worried): Steve, honey, are you here?

Fatal Foe pulls Steve's body parts out to the lonely, dark woods. Crystal, putting on her house robe, heads downstairs to see about Steve.

Crystal, creeping, looks into the kitchen to find mud prints and blood on the floor.

Crystal: Oh my God! Steve, where are you? Did you hurt yourself? Crystal walks out the door of the kitchen into the backyard and toward the woods. Fatal Foe is on the side of the cabin.

He sees Crystal and decapitates her, leaving her body standing headless. Her blood is squirting from her neck all over the place. Fatal Foe waits for her body to drop, takes her body and head, and places them in the woods. The group awakens in the morning. And everyone meets downstairs.

Bob: Hey, you guys! Where's Crystal and Steve?

Alice: I'll go knock on the door.

Alice knocks on the door. The door opens, showing an empty room. Alice runs downstairs.

Alice: They're not upstairs.

Bob: I guess they went out last night.

Dave (looking puzzled): I wonder where?

Bob (laughing): Maybe they got a little freaky last night.

Alice: Well, I need some coffee. What about you guys?

Dave: Yes, honey, that sounds good.

Alice enters the kitchen and notices the door open to the back of the kitchen. Alice returns to the living room.

Alice: They left the kitchen door open. They should have closed it. We could have frozen to death last night.

Dave: They should be back shortly.

Lorraine: Well, I hope so. The girls have to go into town to get beer and groceries for the party. Bob (looking surprised): Damn! That's right, today

is Halloween.

Alice and Lorraine get dressed for their trip into town. They grab their pocketbooks and proceed downstairs to get the car keys.

Alice: Dave, let me have the keys. We're going into town to pick up something. If Crystal comes back, tell her to stay right here.

Alice gets the keys from Dave. Alice and Lorraine get into the Dodge Ram and start their trip into town.

INT... Back at the cabin...

Bob (worrying): This isn't like Steve to run off with some chick.

Dave (joking): Maybe the sex got to his head and now he's playing Romeo or some shit.

Bob: Yeah, maybe you're right, I'm not going to let them blow my high or my holiday. Hell no!

The girls get into town. A strange car is in the shopping mart parking lot, which holds Death Jones in it. He's watching Alice, his long-loved and hated niece. He's breathing hard and his front windshield fogs up as he watches the girls enter the store. The girls are now in the store.

INT... In the shopping mart...

Alice: Well, let's get some chips. What kind do you prefer?

Lorraine: Well, I like Doritos, barbecue, and corn chips.

Alice: What about plain chips and popcorn? Lorraine: See, I like flavor in everything I eat. Alice (looking offended): Well, excuse me.

Lorraine: You know I'm a soul sister, and you are my sister also.

Alice: Okay, let's get some Heinekens. You didn't know I was down.

Lorraine (with pride): I know, baby, I only roll with the best.

The girls pick up several items and head for the counter. Alice pays, and their groceries are bagged. The girls grab their bags and proceed out of the store. Walking through the parking lot and getting back into the jeep, they notice this white-masked man looking their way.

Lorraine (a little nervous): Damn! You see that freak- ass man looking at us?

Alice (brushing it off): I guess he's starting his Halloween a little early today.

Lorraine: I hope I don't have to whip his ass.

Alice (pushing Lorraine into the jeep): Girl, get in! Alice starts up the jeep. The girls lock the doors and drive off. While driving. Alice looks through her rearview mirror and sees the car following them. She pays it no mind. She turns up the music. She and Lorraine are singing and driving, not knowing that Death Jones will follow them to their destination. The girls are almost back to the cabin. Bob and Dave are discussing tonight's events. INT... Back at the cabin...

Bob: Yeah, after the bitch drink, I'm going to get my penis sucked so good that she's going to have twins in her throat.

Dave (looking disgusted): I thought you would have more respect for Lorraine than that.

Bob: I do have respect for my nuts. She loves them; she loves me.

The group is enjoying themselves. Bob and Dave are in the upstairs bedroom smoking pot.

Dave (mumbling with smoke in his mouth): Alice thinks I stopped smoking pot three months ago, and you have me smoking this shit.

Bob (looks serious): I don't have you doing a damn thing. You are your own man. You can pass it back if you feel like that.

Alice comes upstairs and catches Dave passing Bob the pot joint.

Alice (very upset): Damn! Dave, I thought I could trust you. You have absolutely nothing better to do than fry your brain cells.

Dave (apologetic): Alice, I sincerely apologize. Alice (stubborn): I don't want to hear it.

Alice runs down the stairs. Dave attempts to go after Alice, but Bob intervenes, jumping in front of Dave.

Bob: Damn, are you whipped, man? Who wears the pants in your relationship? Come on, let's go fishing

Bob and Dave head downstairs, entering the living room.

Dave: Alice, can I go fishing with Bob?

Alice (acting funny): My opinion doesn't make a difference. Go ahead.

Bob (mumbling in Dave's ear): Did Mommy say you could go?

Dave (pushing Bob away): Knock it off, Bob! Let's go.

Bob and Dave walk out of the cabin.

Lorraine (looks curious): Alice, what was that about?

Alice (seeming upset): Don't worry about it. Just leave it alone.

Bob and Dave walk through the woods in the direction of the lake.

Bob (remembering): Oh shit! After all that fussing. We forgot our beers.

Dave: I'll jog back to the cabin, get the beers, and meet you at the lake.

Bob: You better jog your ass to the lake, because Alice won't allow you back out tonight. I'll go and get the beers.

Dave: Man, you got jokes

Bob is laughing as he walks back toward the cabin. Dave pulls a clipped joint out of his pocket, smoking it as he walks toward the boat, talking to himself....

Dave: I'm going to enjoy myself. Fuck that college bitch, her pussy isn't good anyway.

Dave walks toward the boat. He sees Crystal's headless body in the boat. Dave takes two steps backwards, and Steve's head rolls across Dave's foot. Dave screams as he turns around. Dave and Death Jones are face-to-face. Death Jones lifts Dave up by his neck. Dave's feet are dangling. Death Jones has Dave against a tree, strangling him with one hand. Death Jones takes out his machete and cuts out Dave's large intestines. Death Jones ties Dave to a tree using Dave's large intestines to do so. Bob leaves out the front door of the cabin. Bob is now walking through the woods with the cooler in his hand. From a distance, Bob sees Dave in a tree, slumped over.

Bob (yelling): Damn, Dave, you haven't started fishing yet? You're a lazy motherfucker. Did you have too much to drink?

As Bob gets closer, Bob looks at Dave. Bob: Hey, do you hear me?

As Bob proceeds to get closer to Dave, Bob looks shocked. Bob drops the cooler, walking backward to the boat. Bob stumbles over Steve's head and falls into the boat on top of Crystal's headless body. Bob is hysterical and is screaming. Bob falls out of the boat into the water. Bob gets up, scrambling for his life. Running and screaming through the woods toward the cabin, Bob slams the door and locks it. Bob is breathing hard, looking out the window.

Lorraine (looking curiously at Bob): What's the matter, Bob? Looks like you've seen a ghost.

Alice: Where's Dave? And why are you acting like this? Aren't you guys supposed to be fishing?

Bob (in panic): His head! The tree! Lorraine (intervening): Calm down!

Bob (upset): Bitch, calm down! Give me the keys.

Lorraine: Keys to what? Dave has the keys.

Bob: Dave, Steve, and Crystal-they're all dead by the lake.

Alice: What do you mean they're all dead? Bob (yelling): They're all chopped up. I don't know what the fuck happened out there.

Alice (worried): I'm calling the police!

Alice gets the phone in the kitchen. Alice picks up the receiver and finds out the lines are dead. The lines have been cut. Alice turns around to the group.

Alice: The phone lines are dead.

Lorraine pulls out a cell phone.

Lorraine: This is modern technology. Here, Bob, you call them since you've seen the bodies.

Bob dials 911.

Phone operator: Hello, police. What is your emergency?

Bob: We need the police out here at Camp Crystal Lake.

Bob (upset): Look, that's what I said, and I mean fast as hell

Police operator: Sir, is this a prank call?

Bob (yelling): No. Bitch, all my friends are dead!

Police operator: Sir, please watch your mouth. Crystal Lake was closed down years ago. What are you doing there?

Bob (calming down): I know it's supposed to be closed, but we're here and need help.

Police operator: There are no cars in the area. We'll be there as soon as possible.

Bob hangs up the phone.

Alice: What did they say?

Bob (not satisfied): Not much of nothing, but we have to get the hell out of here.

Lorraine (questioning): How are we going to leave if Dave has the key?

Bob: I wasn't a street hustler for nothing. I'm going to hot wire it. You girls wait for me upstairs, and don't lock the door.

The girls go upstairs, hugging each other, crying and praying. Bob runs to the jeep to find the door locked. Bob picks up a brick and breaks the driver's window. The jeep's alarm goes off. Bob climbs into the seat, snatching out the ignition. Fatal Foe is at the boat looking at Dave's body in the tree. Fatal Foe is holding Dave's pale face. Fatal Foe hears the jeep's alarm and proceeds toward the sound. Bob is fiercely trying to start the jeep. Bob's body is down below the steering wheel. Without Bob realizing it, Fatal Foe takes his hand and grabs Bob's hair, pulling his head into the pane of the window. Fatal Foe takes his machete, and with one strong blow, he cuts Bob's head completely off. Bob's head hits the ground, while the headless body slumps down in the jeep.

Lorraine (worried): Alice, hold this phone. If I'm not back in five minutes, call the cops again. Let me see what happened to Bob.

Alice (afraid): Please don't leave me.

Lorraine: Girl, I'll be right back.

As the girls are talking death, Jones is at the back of the window. Lorraine leaves the cabin. Alice locks the front door of the cabin. Lorraine walks slowly toward the jeep, calling Bob's name. Lorraine thinks Fatal Foe is Bob. Fatal Foe's back is turned to her. Lorraine sees a bloody machete in his hand. As Fatal Foe turns around, Lorraine starts to scream, running toward the cabin. Lorraine gets to the cabin door, banging on it. Alice looks through the window and sees Fatal For coming toward the cabin. Alice runs downstairs. to help Lorraine. As soon as Alice gets to the door, a bloody machete comes though the door and is pulled back out. Fatal Foe had plunged the machete through Lorraine's mouth, which went through the back of her head, through the cabin door. Alice jumps back, screaming. Alice hears the kitchen window break. Death Jones dives through the window. Alice is screaming as she sees Death Jones walk through the kitchen. Alice is screaming, walking backwards. She throws the phone at Death Jones as she runs toward the door. When Alice opens the door, Lorraine's body fall inside the cabin. Alice backs up, screaming. As Death Jones lifts his machete, Fatal Foe walks in the door. Death Jones lowers his arm, which holds the machete. Alice faints; Death Jones and Fatal Foe are looking at each other. Death Jones and Fatal Foe are face to face. Death Jones runs the machete through Fatal Foe's stomach. Fatal Foe drops his machete and grabs Death Jones by the neck with both hands, lifting him off his feet. Fatal Foe throws him through the cabin wall.

Fatal Foe pulls the machete out of his stomach. Fatal Foe walks through the hole in the cabin. Fatal Foe is standing there with his machete in his hand. Death Jones stands up, looking at Fatal Foe, nodding his head side to side, almost amazed at Fatal Foe's strength. Death Jones tackles Fatal Foe through the hole of the cabin wall. Both Death Jones and Fatal Foe land outside of the cabin onto the porch. The noise wakes up Alice, and Alice gets up off the floor and runs to a nearby corner in the living room. Alice is sitting in the corner in a fetal position, holding her knees. Alice watches Fatal Foe and Death Jones fight. Death Jones and Fatal Foe are rolling back and forth on the floor. Death Jones is now sitting on top of Fatal Foe with his hands locked together, bashing Fatal Foe in the face repeatedly. Fatal Foe reaches for the machete that lies on the floor nearby. Fatal Foe stabs Death Jones in the ribs. Death Jones rolls off of Fatal Foe. Death Jones is standing up holding his side. Fatal Foe gets up, swinging the machete at Death Jones. Death Jones is jumping back, waving the blade. Alice gets up and runs out the door. Alice gets to the jeep outside, only to find Bob's headless body slumped over. She moves back from the jeep hysterically. As she walks backwards, someone grabs her. Alice began screaming, until she realizes it's the cops. The cops turn Alice around.

Cops: What's going on in there?

Alice (in shock): The men are fighting in the cabin.

As the police are questioning Alice, Fatal Foe gets thrown out of the window. Cops: Oh shit!

The cops draw their weapons Cops: What the hell is that?

Fatal Foe is lying there four feet from the window. Death Jones comes climbing out the window, holding the machete in his hand.

Cops (yelling): Hold it right there!

Death Jones continues to walk toward Fatal Foe, and the cops shoot Death Jones, emptying their weapons. Death Jones drops beside Fatal Foe. Death Jones and Fatal Foe are lying on the porch side by side.

Cops: Miss, please stay right here.

The cops walk over to Death Jones and Fatal Foe, checking for their pulses. As the cops check both of their pulses, Fatal Foe grabs one by the neck, and Death Jones grabs the other cop's neck, strangling both officers and crushing their necks. Both officers are now dead. Fatal Foe and Death Jones stand up, continuing to fight. A car pulls up behind Alice. It's her father, Tommy. Alice stands there in shock.

Tommy: Alice, baby, I tried to call you; the lines were dead. What's going on here?

Alice (in shock): He's here. Tommy: Who?

Tommy looks over and sees Fatal Foe and Death Jones wrestling on the cabin porch. With a violent shove, Fatal Foe throws Death Jones straight through the cabin wall. Then, Fatal Foe's gaze locks onto Alice and Tommy. He steps off the porch and starts toward them.

Tommy grabs Alice's hand and pulls her toward the car. He reaches inside and pulls out a shotgun. He pumps it, but the gun jams. Before Fatal Foe can reach them, Death Jones staggers back out of the wreckage. With a guttural roar, he swings his machete, slicing Fatal Foe's head clean off. The body crashes to the ground right in front of Alice and Tommy, blood pooling at their feet.

Death Jones stands in full view, his machete dripping, his eyes locked on them. Tommy grips the shotgun tightly, takes Alice's hand, and pulls her toward the cabin. Death Jones follows at a slow, deliberate pace—moving like a dead man who can't be stopped.

Tommy and Alice rush through the cabin's broken front and slip out the back. They creep to the side, watching Death Jones approach the porch again. His movements are eerie, unnatural, like something risen from the grave.

Tommy pushes Alice back.

Tommy: Baby, stay right here.

Tommy steps out from the side of the cabin.

Tommy (yelling): Death Jones!

The monster turns his head, nodding side to side like a predator scenting blood. He lumbers toward Tommy. Tommy raises the shotgun, fires, and blasts into Death Jones's chest. The shot tears through him, but he keeps moving. Another shot rings out—this time hitting his shoulder, staggering him. Finally, a third shot lands square in his torso, sending him collapsing in flames of blood and smoke.

Death Jones takes a few more staggering steps before falling face-first into the dirt.

Alice breaks down, hysterical and crying. Tommy drops the shotgun, takes her hand, and pulls her into an embrace. Father and daughter walk back to the car together. They climb inside, shaken but alive.

Tommy: Well, baby, it's been a nightmare, but it's

over.

Alice: That sounds like a dream.

Tommy: Baby, it's always been a nightmare.

Back near the cabin, Death Jones's body lies there lifelessly. Within seconds, Death Jones's left arm rises up in the air and then drops.